for Stevie

First published by Walker Books Ltd.
87 Vauxhall Walk, London SE11 5HJ

First U.S. edition 2003

Library of Congress Cataloging-in-Publication Data is available.
Library of Congress Catalog Card Number 2003043852

ISBN 0-7636-2195-1

2 4 6 8 10 9 7 5 3 1

Printed in China

This book was hand lettered by the artist.
The illustrations were done in gouache.

Candlewick Press
2067 Massachusetts Avenue
Cambridge, Massachusetts 02140

visit us at www.candlewick.com

# Maisy's Rainbow Dream

Lucy Cousins

CANDLEWICK PRESS
CAMBRIDGE, MASSACHUSETTS

maisy is fast asleep
in her little bed.
Suddenly a dream begins
inside her head.

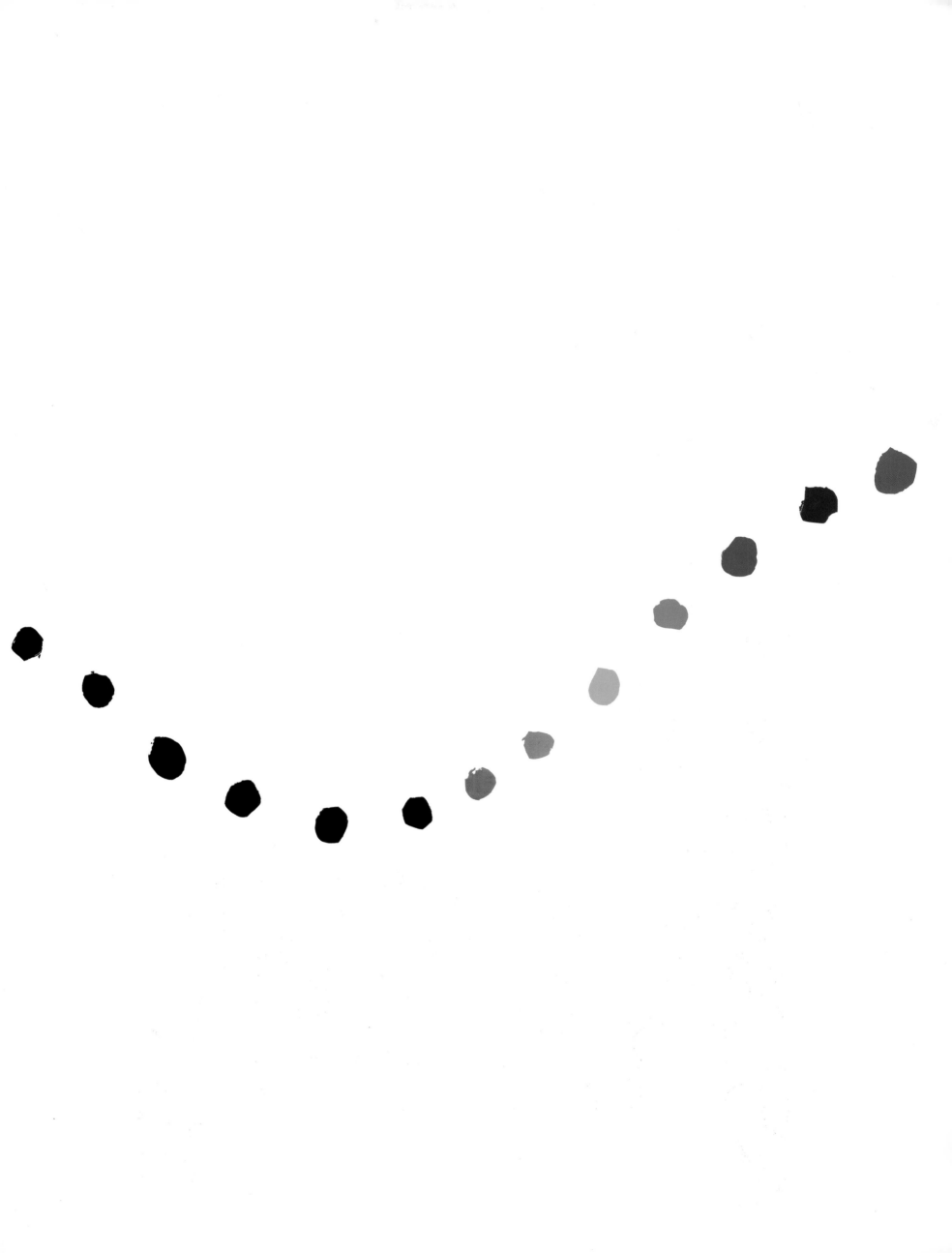

Maisy dreams she is going on a journey. Her friends are coming too.

maisy dreams
about a
red ladybug.

# Maisy dreams about an Orange fish.

maisy dreams
about a
yellow bee.

Maisy dreams about a green leaf.

Maisy dreams about a blue clock.

maisy dreams
about
indigo spots.

maisy dreams about a violet butterfly.

maisy dreams she's arrived in Rainbowland.

Maisy wakes up from her rainbow dream. Good morning, Maisy. It's a beautiful day!

# CREATION

## Gerald McDermott

**Dutton Children's Books**

**New York**

For Candace, Raye, and Josh

Text and illustrations copyright © 2003 by Gerald McDermott
All rights reserved

CIP Data is available.

Published in the United States by Dutton Children's Books,
a division of Penguin Young Readers Group
345 Hudson Street, New York, N.Y. 10014
www.penguin.com

First Edition
ISBN 0-525-46905-2
10 9 8 7 6 5 4 3 2 1

Typography designed by Joy Chu
Manufactured in China

## AUTHOR'S NOTE

These words and images grew out of my desire to cast in a new light the often-told and much beloved story of creation and to welcome everyone, regardless of the direction from which they come, to enter into this ancient mystery with an open heart. The voice of the story is an inner one that begins with a breath and a whisper, a spark ignited within us all that grows to illuminate the universe.

My telling is based on Genesis 1:1 through 2:3 of the Hebrew Bible, with an eye toward its antecedents in the ancient Near East, such as the Babylonian epic *Enuma Elish,* and sources as diverse as the illuminated *Bibles Moralisées* of thirteenth-century France and the Sarajevo Haggadah of fourteenth-century Spain.

A long journey—figuratively through the stories of many different cultures and literally far from home—gave me new perspectives. I conceived the words in Santiago de Chile and sketched the first images in Tokyo. I returned from Japan with a portfolio of handmade mulberry-bark paper whose organic textures inspired the swirls and shadings of my gesso-and-fabric color paintings. As in all of my work, *Creation* is an outer expression of the inner reality that connects every human soul.

GRATEFUL ACKNOWLEDGMENTS TO STEPHANIE OWENS LURIE, JOY CHU, SANDRA GORDON, AND JASON WARE.
—G.M.

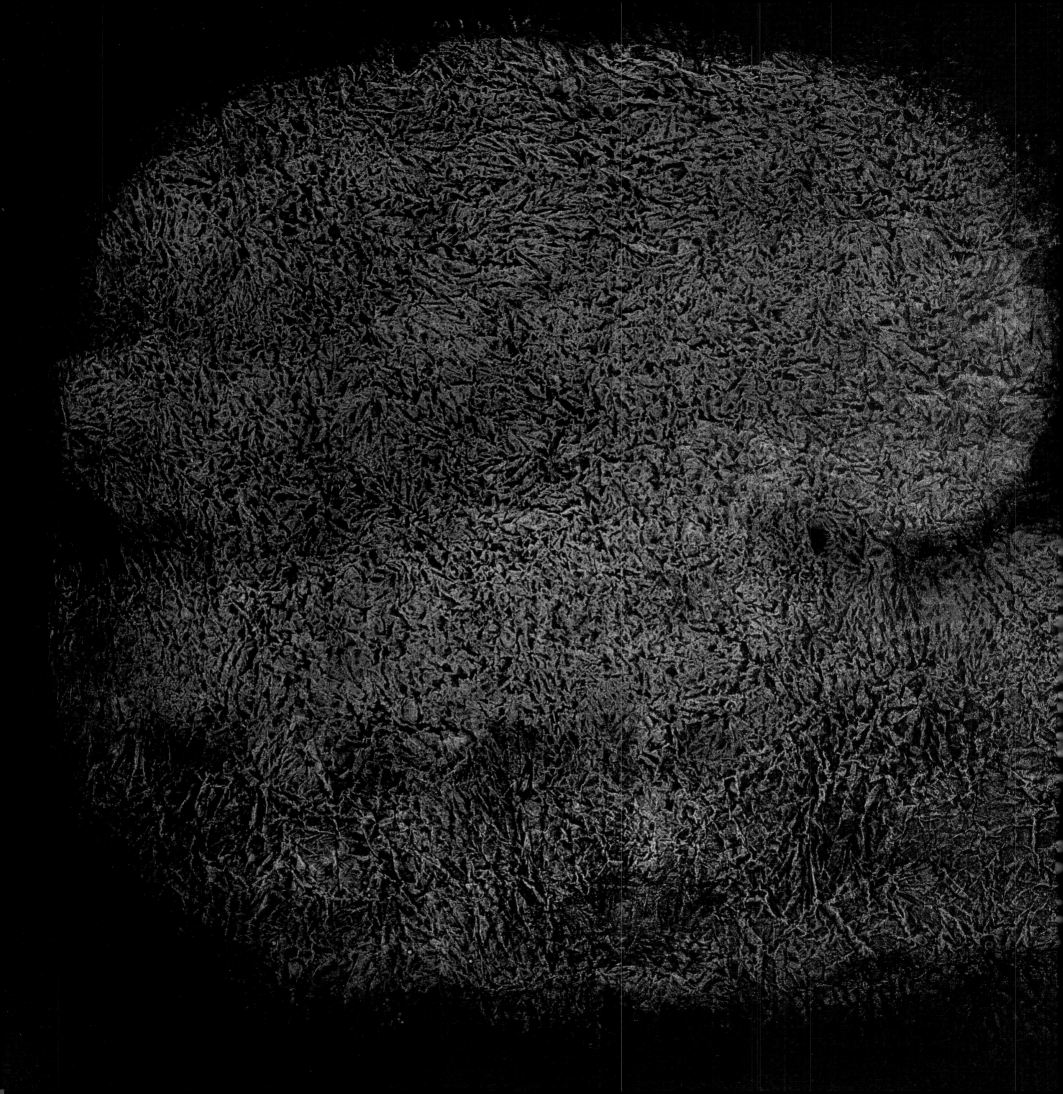

I was before time.
I was everywhere.
There was nothing.
I was there.
My spirit moved over the deep.
I floated in darkness.

Then I breathed light
into the dark.

The light became day.

The darkness became **night.**

I divided the **mists,** sweet and salt.
**There was water above.**
**There was water below.**

Between them was heaven.

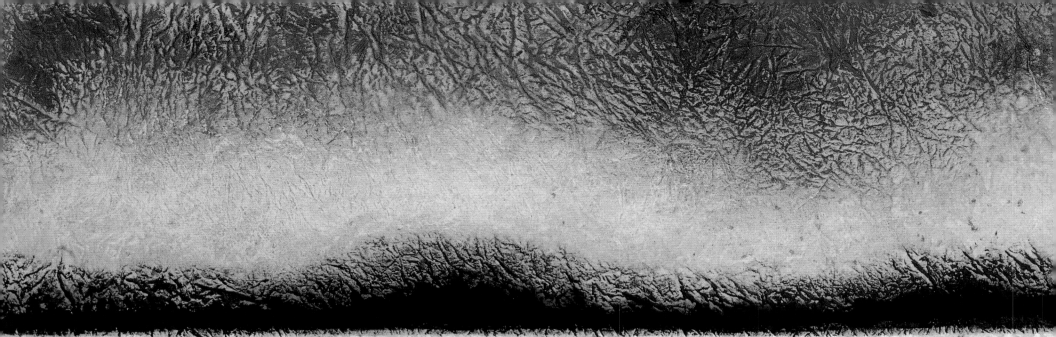

I gathered together
the waters below
and made the sea.

Out of the sea
I brought the earth.

Out of the earth I brought
grasses and herbs,
**seeds** and **roots**,
flowers, **trees**,
and **fruit**.

I put **shining lights** in **heaven.**

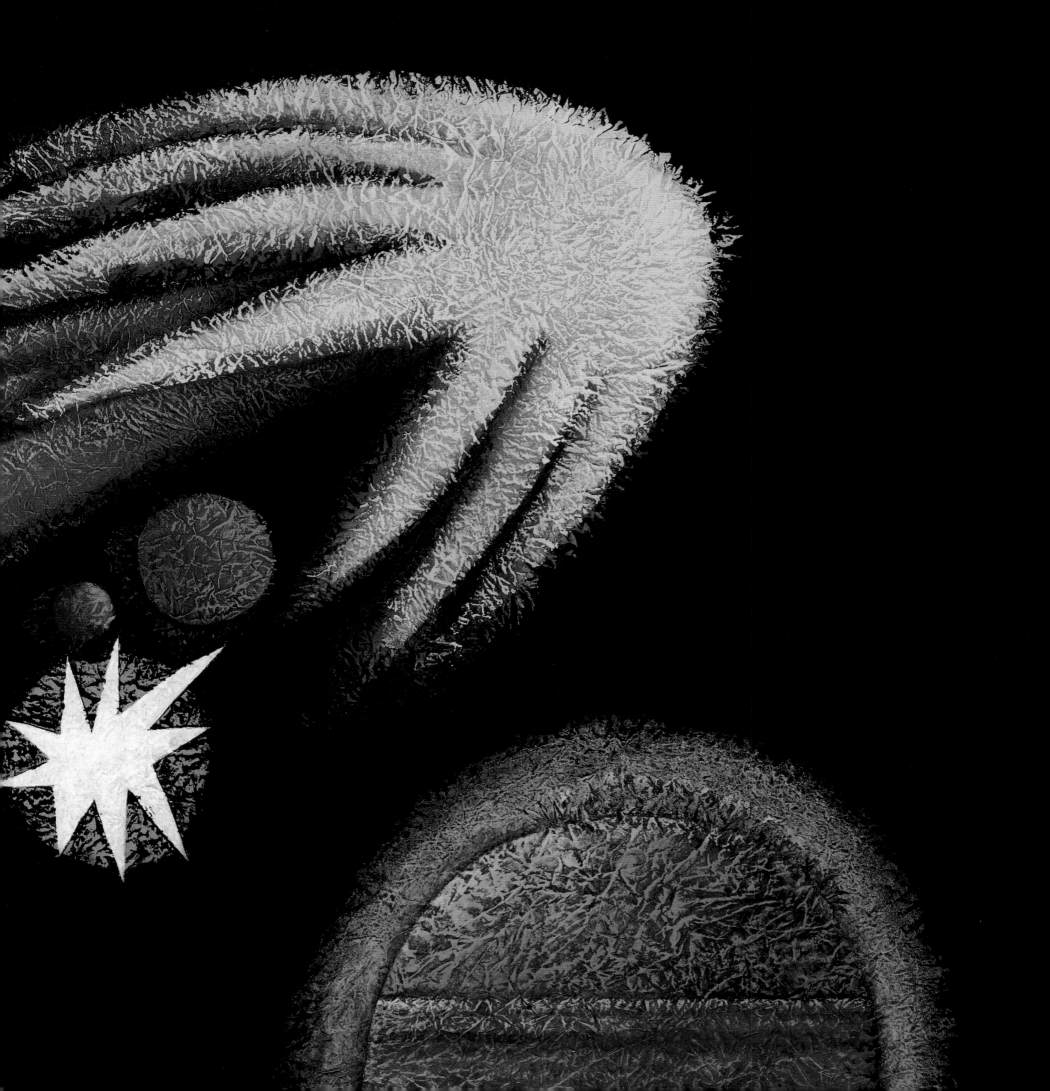

The great light is the **sun.**
The small light is the **moon.**
The smallest lights are the **stars.**

Sun, moon, stars.

These signs mark the seasons.

Between **heaven** and **earth**
my spirit soared on the **wings of birds.**
My creatures began to **fill the world.**

They swam in the **sea.**

They crawled in the grass.

They moved over the earth.

Out of **myself** I brought
**man** and **woman**.
I gave my gifts to them.
They would be the keepers
of all this beauty.

Darkness, **mist**, water, light.
Seed, root, flower, **tree**,
and **fruit**.

Sun, moon, stars.

Creatures that swim.
Creatures that crawl.
Creatures that fly.
Creatures that move
over the earth
with **woman and man**
to care for them.

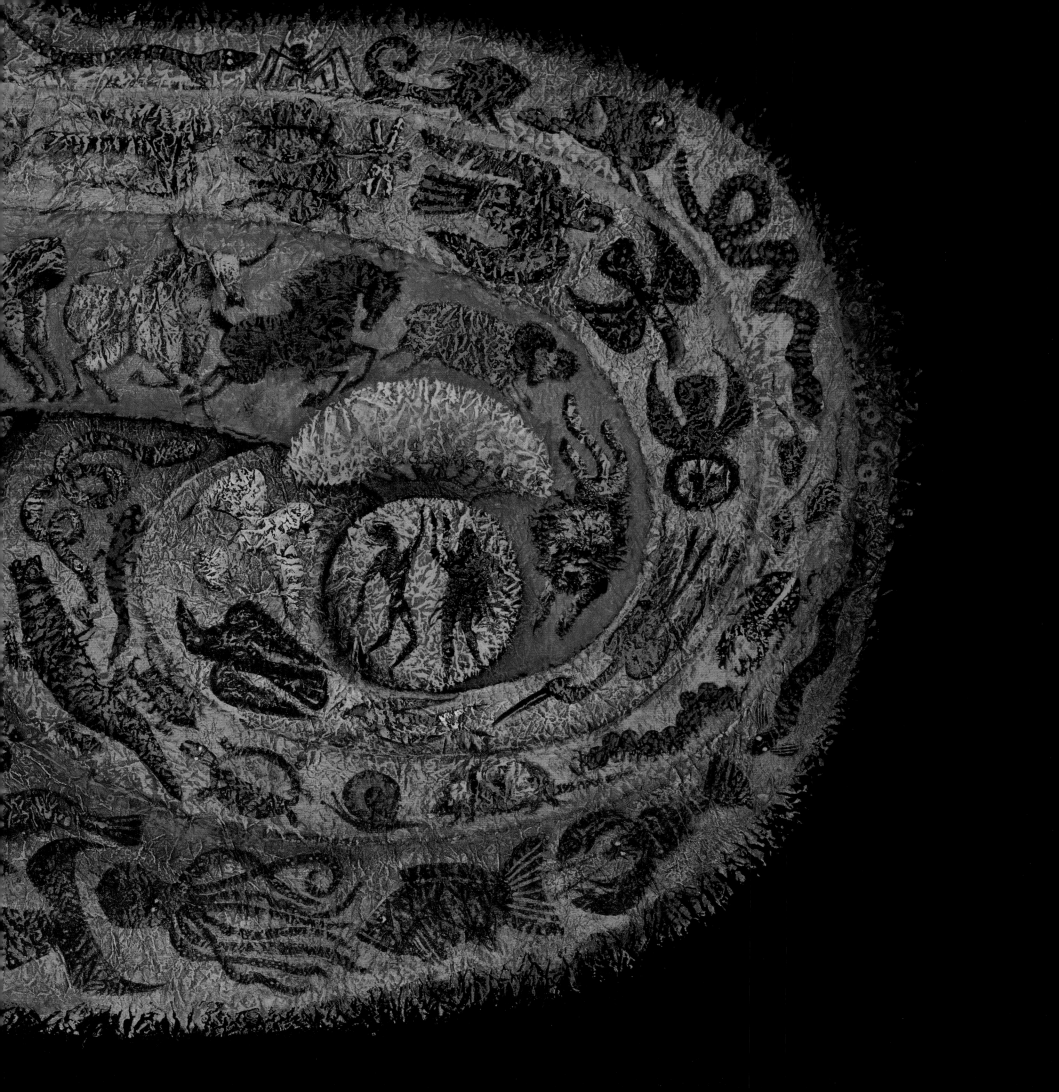

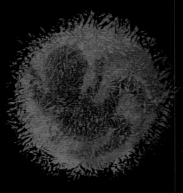

I am all this.
**All this I AM.**